Contents

Swashbuckle School

Collect all six exciting adventures:

Scarlet SILVER

Swashbuckle School

Original concept by Sarah McConnell
Written by Lucy Courtenay
Illustrations by Sarah McConnell

Hodder
Children's
Books

A division of Hachette Children's Books

First published in Great Britain in 2009
by Hodder Children's Books

ISBN: 978 0 340 98912 8 (HB)
ISBN: 978 0 340 95967 1 (PB)

Printed in Great Britain by
Clays Ltd, St Ives plc

The paper and board used in this paperback by Hodder Children's Books
are natural recyclable products made from wood grown in
sustainable forests. The manufacturing processes conform to the
environmental regulations of the country of origin.

Hodder Children's Books
a division of Hachette Children's Books
338 Euston Road, London NW1 3BH
An Hachette Livre UK Company

www.hachettelivre.co.uk

The First Voyage

Once upon a glittering ocean, there was a pirate ship.

She didn't look much like a pirate ship. She had flowery window boxes and a tiled roof. Peeping out of the water was the top half of a red front door. There was a large pair of pants on the washing line and a plate of half-eaten sandwiches on the deck. But she *was* a pirate ship, and her name was *55 Ocean Drive*.

High up in the crow's nest of *55 Ocean Drive*, a small blonde pirate in a purple pirate hat stared out to sea through her silver telescope.

"Nothing out there, Bluebeard," Scarlet Silver sighed.

"Sufferin' seagulls," grumbled Bluebeard the budgie from his perch on Scarlet's hat.

Scarlet stroked Bluebeard's ruffled feathers. Then she folded up her telescope and put it in her pocket. She looked down at the deck of *55 Ocean Drive* and almost burst with pride. Her first pirate voyage at last! She could hardly believe it.

Suddenly the ship veered sharply to the left. Scarlet lost her balance and shot out of the crow's nest. She clung on with one finger as Bluebeard flapped around her head.

The deck was a long way down.

"Mum!" Scarlet shouted.

A red-haired lady in a stylish blue sweater dress was holding the ship's wheel. She peered up at Scarlet in alarm. "Sorry," said Lila Silver, adjusting her glasses. "I was trying a three-point turn. It went a bit wrong at two and a half."

"You're not driving your old sports car now, Mum," said Scarlet, still dangling from the crow's nest. "This is a pirate ship, remember?"

"Hold on, darling," said Lila. "I'll come and get you."

"Whatever you do," Scarlet began.

Lila let go of the wheel.

"… please don't let go of the wheel," Scarlet finished.

55 Ocean Drive swung around. Scarlet

felt her finger slipping as Lila rushed to grab the wheel again.

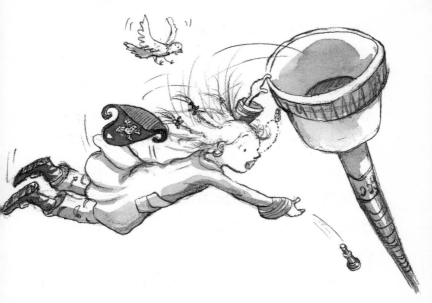

With a mighty effort, Scarlet stretched out her free hand. She gripped the edge of the crow's nest and pulled herself up. It was too late to save her hat and her telescope, which had already hit the deck.

"Wow," said Bluebeard.

13

"Right!" Scarlet shouted from the crow's nest when she'd got her breath back. "Back to work, crew. The mainsail needs hoisting. The poop deck needs scrubbing."

"The *poop* deck?" Cedric Silver gave a snigger.

Scarlet sighed. "Yes, little brother," she said. "The poop deck."

"Well, I'm not doing it," Cedric said. "I'm busy."

"You're polishing your space helmet," Scarlet said. "That doesn't count, Cedric."

Cedric took off his bandana and forced his space helmet down over his glasses. He tied his bandana around his helmet and shut his visor. "The name is Space Beard, not Cedric," he said in a muffly voice. "The pirate astronaut of the Seven

Seas. Off to fight pirate aliens, garr, take me to your leader."

Cedric was crazy about space. He knew about planets and black holes, and wanted a telescope that was bigger than *55 Ocean Drive*. Scarlet sometimes wondered if Cedric was an alien just *pretending* to be her brother.

"Stupid space-face," Scarlet muttered.

Cedric flipped up his space visor. "What?"

Scarlet smiled sweetly. "Nothing."

She stared at the empty mainmast. They had to hoist the mainsail soon, or

55 Ocean Drive would drift back into shore.

There's no way, thought Scarlet, *that my first pirate voyage is going to wash up on a beach by mistake.*

"Hoist the mainsail!" Scarlet shouted. "Man the wheel!"

The enormous pile of sailcloth on the deck of *55 Ocean Drive* fell over with a thump. A skinny man with a twisty moustache and straw-like hair crawled out of the sails and rubbed his head.

"Ouch," said Melvin Silver. "Which one is the mainsail again?"

"I still have the wheel," said Lila. "But I'm not a man."

The sea sloshed up the sides of *55 Ocean Drive* and washed away two window boxes. The Silvers' cat Ralph, who had been washing his bottom on a

16

window sill, shot up a nearby mast.

"Whee," Lila giggled.

Scarlet groaned.

Her family just didn't get it. They were supposed to be *pirates*.

Until yesterday, the Silvers hadn't even realised they *were* pirates. This was something Scarlet had never understood. With a notorious pirate granny like Long Joan Silver, of *course* they were pirates.

Long Joan Silver had been as famous as the ocean was wide. With her bright pink frock coats, high-heeled pirate boots and collection of multi-coloured mascaras, pirate captains all over the world had fallen in love with her – and then not noticed as she pinched their treasure.

Old pirates still went misty at the
mention of her name. As Cedric put it,
she had been one interstellar granny.

But all that had changed when Long
Joan disappeared.

The Silvers lived aboard Long Joan's

old pirate ship, *55 Ocean Drive*. Of course, *55 Ocean Drive* hadn't always been called *55 Ocean Drive*. It had once been known as the *Slinky Stocking*. One terrible day, the *Slinky Stocking* had sailed home with the news that Long Joan Silver and her faithful parrot Lipstick had been eaten by a giant shrimp. Without their captain, the crew didn't want to be pirates any more. They ran the *Slinky Stocking* aground at the bottom of a road of fifty-four houses and one lamp-post.

The road was called Ocean Drive. So the *Slinky Stocking* was forgotten, and *55 Ocean Drive* was born. A front door was added. Washing began to dangle from the rigging. And in the Silver household, no one in the family was ever allowed to mention pirates again.

Until Scarlet found gold in the garden.

Pirate fever broke out. There was no turning back as the Silvers dug out the garden of *55 Ocean Drive* like – well, like pirates. They dug so deep that *55 Ocean Drive* fell back into the sea and that, as they say, was that.

The Silvers were pirates through and through, and it was time they realised it.

All her life, Scarlet had wanted to be a pirate. She had read all of Long Joan's diaries and pirate books. Every day she had practised swinging on the ropes of *55 Ocean Drive* and climbing to the top of the mainmast with a blindfold on. Every night she had practised spitting and cleaning her teeth with a knife (until her mum had taken the knife away). She knew lots of rude pirate curses. She owned four pirate hats in different colours, and her room was decorated from top to bottom with treasure maps. Now *55 Ocean Drive* was afloat again, Scarlet had everything she needed to become a famous pirate just like her grandmother.

Except a decent pirate crew.

Scarlet grabbed a rope and swung down on to the deck. Then she did a quick pirate cartwheel. Her beaded plaits went *clackety-clack* as she landed on her feet and folded her arms. Bluebeard settled on her hat.

"You lot need pirate lessons," Scarlet announced.

"Good idea," said Melvin. "Let's ask Grandpa Jack to teach us. He was

married to Long Joan
for forty years.
He must
have picked
up a few tips."

"No," Scarlet said.
"*I'm* going to—"

"Mum!" Cedric shouted
from the prow of the ship.
"Fishing boat ahead!"

Lila pulled on the wheel of *55
Ocean Drive*. There was a crunch
and a yell.

Cedric flipped up his space visor
and peered into the water.

"The other way would have been
better," Cedric said.

"Oops," Lila said.

"Those fishermen are waving at us,"
Melvin said. "Let's wave back."

Scarlet put her head in her hands.
"They aren't waving, Dad," she said.
"Look. You really, really need pirate
lessons. I know just the person to teach
you. And it's not Grandpa Jack."

Grandpa Jack was apologising to the
three fishermen, whom he knew from the
local fishing club. He was a keen
fisherman himself and spent hours with
his fishing rod, catching stones and
mackerel and shopping trolleys

for the family to eat. (They generally just ate the mackerel.) When he wasn't fishing, Grandpa Jack liked knitting large jumpers for everyone to wear. The Silvers were quite relieved when he went back to fishing again.

"The obvious choice is—" continued Scarlet.

"How about One-Eyed Scott?" Lila said. "He sailed in Long Joan's pirate crew."

Everyone looked at the skinny old ex-pirate fishing beside Grandpa Jack. One-Eyed Scott was Grandpa Jack's best friend. He had a shiny eye patch and chicken bones tied in his thinning black hair. Scarlet had learned some of her best pirate curses from One-Eyed Scott. But One-Eyed Scott was getting old. His elbows hurt and his knees creaked and even his one eye wasn't up to much.

Scarlet stamped her foot. "Not Grandpa Jack, you lolloping loonies," she said. "Not One-Eyed Scott either. *I'm* the best pirate on this ship, so *I'm* going to teach you. Got it?"

"You'd better be quick," Cedric said.

"I know," Scarlet sighed. "I hardly know where to begin, to be honest."

"Could you begin with something useful?" Lila said. "Like, what to do when you are attacked?"

There was a horrible shout behind Scarlet.

"AAARRRGGGHHH!!!"

Scarlet leaped out of her skin.

A dozen pirates had jumped on to the deck of *55 Ocean Drive*.

And they didn't look friendly.

Captain Scarlet

Scarlet stared at the invaders. Where had they come from? She made a note in her head. *Never take your eyes off the horizon.*

The pirate chief swaggered forward. His shiny hair curled down to his shoulders. He held his three-cornered hat in one hand. His purple cloak had a picture on it, of a pirate glove clutching a pile of banknotes. His boots were shiny and his cutlass looked sharp.

"My name is Captain Curl," sneered the pirate chief. He flipped his curls over his shoulders. "Who is the captain of this vessel?"

"We don't have a captain," said Lila.

It was true. Although Scarlet *felt* like the captain, the family hadn't voted for a captain yet. And pirates *always* voted for their captains.

"No captain?" repeated Captain Curl.

"No captain?" repeated his crew.

The invaders started laughing. Not having a captain was obviously the funniest joke they'd heard in months.

"We work as a team," Lila said.

Scarlet and Cedric rolled their eyes. Teamwork was one of their mother's favourite subjects.

"Teamwork isn't something you would

know about," Lila continued. "You should be ashamed of yourselves, creeping up on us like that."

"Mum," Scarlet muttered. "They're pirates. It's what pirates *do*." She tried to think of something extremely clever and piratey that might save them. Her brain felt like fudge.

Captain Curl came a little closer. His teeth glinted with gold fillings. His breath stank of rotten biscuits.

At last, Scarlet had an idea.

"Jump!" she shouted.

And she jumped straight up into the rigging with a whoop.

Melvin had been an acrobat before Scarlet was born. So he jumped like he was on springs, with a somersault in the middle. Lila and Cedric jumped as well.

For a moment, Scarlet thought Cedric wasn't going to make it … but then Lila reached out her hand and pulled Cedric up behind her.

Grandpa Jack and One-Eyed Scott climbed the mizzen mast at the back of the ship. Grandpa Jack was panting, and Ralph the cat was sitting on his head. One-Eyed Scott was still holding his fishing rod.

Balancing on the yardarm, Scarlet looked down at the invaders. From up here, she could see a bald patch on the top of Captain Curl's curly head.

"So," Scarlet said. "Did a parrot peck out your hair?"

Captain Curl turned purple.

"Come down and say that, missy," he bellowed.

"No thanks," Scarlet said. "The view's better up here."

Captain Curl tried to swing himself into the rigging.

"If you like bald heads," Scarlet added.

The pirate chief lost his grip. "Nobody jokes about Captain Curl's curls," he roared furiously.

The crew started sniggering.

"Stop sniggering," Captain Curl shouted. He clamped his tricorn hat on to his head. "I'll thrash the lot of you! Sniggering is mutiny!"

"So, Baldie," Scarlet said. "What happens next?"

Captain Curl waved his cutlass. "Come

down and fight!" he yelled.

"Not a chance!" called Grandpa Jack from the mizzen mast.

Scarlet hoped One-Eyed Scott would say something fantastically rude.

"Baboon-bum head," said One-Eyed Scott with a grin.

Now everyone was sniggering.

"Fine," said the pirate chief, trembling with rage. "We'll just starve you down."

"AR!" the crew bellowed happily. "Starve you down!"

"We'll tell our granny on you!" Cedric shouted bravely.

"Ooooh," Captain Curl said. "I'm really scared."

"You should be," said Cedric. "Our granny is Long Joan Silver, terror of the Seven Seas!"

The crew stopped laughing. They gawped at Cedric. Scarlet could hear anxious murmuring.

"Long Joan Silver lies in the belly of a shrimp," Captain Curl smirked. "She can't save you now."

"Oh," said Cedric. "I thought maybe they didn't know."

"It was worth a try," Scarlet said. "Now, how about dropping your space helmet on Captain Curl's head?"

Cedric dropped his space helmet on Captain Curl's head.

WHAM! The pirate chief hit the deck with a surprised *oof*.

"ATTACK!" shouted Scarlet, and jumped down from the yardarm.

"ATTACK!" the rest of the family roared, and jumped down as well.

Grandpa Jack walloped two pirates' heads together. One-Eyed Scott tied up another three with his fishing line. Ralph flew at the invaders with his claws flashing and his tail puffed up like a loobrush. Zooming overhead, Bluebeard screeched "Pieces of eight!" and dropped budgie-poo missiles. Melvin wrapped up two pirates in sailcloth and Lila stuck the heads of two more through the spokes on

the ship's wheel.

"Avast!" Scarlet shouted, whirling pirate kung-fu arms.

Captain Curl woke up. He looked groggily at the fight. A dollop of budgie poo landed on his nose.

"Yuck!" shouted the pirate chief.
"Abandon the fight, men!"

And scrambling to his feet, Captain
Curl jumped over the side of *55 Ocean
Drive*.

The Silvers and One-Eyed Scott pushed

the rest of the pirate crew over the side with a mighty yell.

"The blood of Long Joan Silver lives on!" Scarlet shouted. She put her foot on the ship's railings as the invaders swam feebly for their ship. "Fear the kung-fu arms! Fear the fishing line! Fear the budgie poo!"

"Well done, Captain," Lila said, putting her hand on Scarlet's shoulder. "Your quick thinking saved this ship."

"Captain?" Scarlet gasped. "Me? But we haven't voted!"

"Let's vote now," Lila said. "All those in favour of Scarlet Silver as captain of *55 Ocean Drive*, say aye."

"AYE!" cheered the family.

"Pieces of eight!" Bluebeard screeched.

"Miaow!" said Ralph.

"That's settled then," Lila said.

"Let's have a pirate ceremony," Cedric suggested.

The family gathered on the deck.

"Scarlet Silver," said Lila. "We swear to follow you to the ends of the earth. And we give you the keys to this ship."

Scarlet blushed and twiddled one of her beaded plaits as Melvin handed over the keys to *55 Ocean Drive*. The keyring was made of clear plastic, set around a bright red parrot feather that had once belonged to Lipstick.

"In memory of Long Joan Silver and Lipstick," Lila said, "we elect you … *Captain Scarlet*."

Back to School

"My first job as captain," Scarlet said, "is to say sorry. I took my eyes off the horizon and we were invaded. I don't know as much about pirating as I thought."

"We're all beginners," Melvin said.

"Constipated catfish," One-Eyed Scott said, "I ain't no beginner. I should have known better."

"Me too," said Grandpa Jack.

"You're just out of practice," Lila said.

"It looks like we *all* need pirate lessons," Scarlet said. "We'll be a fantastic pirate crew when we've learned a few more tricks, I'm sure."

"And when I've added some jumping springs to my super splints," Cedric said.

Cedric had been born with wobbly legs. He had worn special leg splints since he was three. He had one pair of splints with aliens on it, and another pair covered in treasure chests. He liked adapting them with gadgets like tin openers and corkscrews.

"But who's going to teach us?" Melvin asked with a frown.

A piece of paper fluttered across the deck. Bluebeard swooped down and caught it in his beak. Then he brought it to Scarlet.

It was a gold-coloured leaflet with a

picture of a pirate glove on it. In big
piratey letters, the leaflet said:

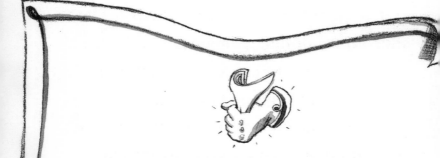

IS YOUR CUTLASS BLUNT?
ARE YOUR PIRATE CURSES LAME?
DOES YOUR BUCKLE LACK SWASH?

COME TO SWASHBUCKLE SCHOOL

AND LEARN FROM THE MASTER,
CAPTAIN GILBERT
GAUNTLET!

APPLICANTS FROM ALL SWIMS
OF LIFE WELCOME!

SWASHBUCKLE SCHOOL IS SITUATED AT
JUNCTION 3 OF THE W40.

FREE MOORING!

"One of the invaders must have dropped it," Cedric said. "The pirate chief had that glove thing on his cloak."

"I've heard of Gilbert Gauntlet," Scarlet said. "But I don't know why."

"Maybe he's an old mate of Long Joan's!" Lila said in excitement.

Melvin dashed into the cabin. He came out with one of Long Joan Silver's old pirate charts. "This is the W40," he said, pointing at a waterway on the chart. "We're here. Swashbuckle School isn't far. Why don't we give it a try?"

Scarlet's head filled with wonderful pirate thoughts. They would learn how to find buried treasure. Scarlet would use a cutlass (Lila had never let her). They would study pirate curses to make One-Eyed Scott blush. Scarlet knew they would come top in all their classes and get a special pirate award.

"What are we waiting for?" Scarlet said, putting the leaflet in her pocket. "Swashbuckle School, here we come!"

Under Scarlet's leadership, *55 Ocean Drive* sailed like the wind. There was plenty of spare time, but the crew kept busy. Grandpa Jack caught seven fish and a sardine tin. With new jumping springs on his splints, Cedric learned to leap into the rigging with one bounce. Lila and Melvin wrote a new pirate song called *The Groovy Groat* and taught Bluebeard to shout "boo-boo be-doo" in the chorus. One-Eyed Scott made up an elbow-waving, shoe-shuffling dance to go with *The Groovy Groat*, and Ralph had

the cleanest bottom on the Seven Seas.

Three days later, they reached the
harbour of Swashbuckle Island. A fishing
boat, a speedboat, a tug and a wonky old
galleon were already moored at the quay.

"Those must belong to the other pirate
trainees," Lila guessed.

"Or maybe Gilbert Gauntlet himself!"
said Cedric.

"Drop anchor!" Scarlet shouted from the crow's nest.

55 Ocean Drive's anchor sploshed into the clear blue water. The Silvers and One-Eyed Scott clattered down the gangplank and on to the quay, where a flashing arrow blinked at them.

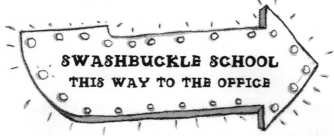

They followed the arrow off the quay and along a sparkling white beach. Palm trees waved overhead. Parrots screeched high up in the branches.

"This is the perfect pirate island," Scarlet sighed happily.

"That must be the office," Melvin said.

The Silvers and One-Eyed Scott stared at the beach hut in front of them. It was bright purple, with a huge golden pirate glove clutching a pile of banknotes painted on the side.

As they watched, loud accordion music blasted across the beach. The doors at one end of the hut banged open. A man with big blond hair and very white teeth stepped on to the sand. He was wearing a pinstriped pirate coat with shiny gold buttons and polished black boots. He held open his arms and smiled.

"Welcome to Swashbuckle School, my hearties," said Gilbert Gauntlet.

Gilbert Gauntlet shook Melvin's hand and stroked Ralph's head. He tickled Bluebeard under the chin. He put his arm around Lila and he talked about

47

fish with Grandpa Jack. He admired the
chicken bones in One-Eyed Scott's hair
and made googly alien eyes at Cedric.

Then he came to Scarlet.

"What a splendid pirate hat, girlie," he said. "It's the perfect colour for you."

"My name isn't girlie," said Scarlet. "It's Scarlet."

She was getting a bad feeling about Gilbert Gauntlet.

Where had she heard his name before?

"Marvellous," Gilbert Gauntlet said, squeezing Scarlet's shoulders.

"Pirates don't say marvellous," Scarlet said with a frown.

The bad feeling was getting worse.

"With my expert help, you're all going to be first-class students at Swashbuckle School," Gilbert Gauntlet said. "You have real pirate style."

Scarlet tried to catch her dad's eye. But Melvin was beaming at Gilbert Gauntlet. So was everyone else.

"The paperwork's in the hut," Gilbert Gauntlet said. "Let's sign the deal!"

"Pirates spit on their palms and shake hands when they make a deal," Scarlet said loudly.

Gilbert Gauntlet looked disgusted. "That's not how we do business *nowadays*," he said, ushering the Silvers and One-Eyed Scott into the beach hut.

Inside, the hut looked like a proper office. It had a computer, a filing cabinet, a swizzly chair and a large desk. Everything was decorated in purple and gold. Lying on the desk was a contract and a parrot-feather quill.

"Dad," said Scarlet.

"Sign here, and here, and here," Gilbert Gauntlet said. He pushed the quill into Melvin's hand.

"Dad?" Scarlet said again, more loudly this time.

"Hmm?" said Melvin. He signed the contract.

"Can I talk to you?" Scarlet said.

"In a minute," Melvin said. "Pass me the keys to *55 Ocean Drive*, will you Scarlet love?"

Reluctantly, Scarlet passed them over. Gilbert Gauntlet hung the plastic-coated red-parrot-feather keyring on a large purple keyboard behind the desk, beside four other keyrings.

They all stepped out of the office. Gilbert Gauntlet pressed a plipper on his own keyring. The doors and shutters of the Swashbuckle School office slammed shut. And suddenly, Scarlet really wished she hadn't given her dad the keys to *55*

Ocean Drive after all.

"The first rule of Swashbuckle School," said Gilbert Gauntlet with a crocodile smile, "is: *always read stuff before you sign it*. You're mine now, my hearties. All mine!"

Lipstick

"I don't understand," Melvin said.

Scarlet made another note in her head. *Always trust your instincts.* She would start her own pirate notes as soon as she got back to *55 Ocean Drive*.

If she ever got back to *55 Ocean Drive*.

"*I* understand," Scarlet said. "You're a crook, Gilbert Gauntlet."

"Of course I'm a crook, girlie," said Gilbert Gauntlet. "I'm a pirate. You met

Captain Curl, did you? I send him out to find pupils for Swashbuckle School. You'll see him later."

"Not all pirates are crooks, you know," Lila said furiously.

"You've signed a contract promising to stay here until I say you can leave," Gilbert Gauntlet said. "Now put your uniforms on."

He handed them T-shirts and caps in

several shades of purple. They all had the familiar pirate glove on them.

Scarlet thought of her fabulous wardrobe on board *55 Ocean Drive*. It was filled with velvet coats, frilled shirts, buckled boots and half a dozen plumes for her pirate hats.

"You want me to wear *that*?" she said in disgust. "But it's like, *gross*."

Five large pirates came out of the palm trees and stood beside Gilbert Gauntlet. They were all wearing purple T-shirts and scary expressions. One of them was Captain Curl. His purple cap covered his bald patch, and his curly brown hair fell in shining waves on his purple shoulders.

"The second rule of Swashbuckle School," said Gilbert Gauntlet, "is always obey the captain. You," he added, pointing at One-Eyed Scott. "Lose the chicken bones. They smell."

"I thought you liked them," said One-Eyed Scott.

"I was lying," Gilbert Gauntlet said. "I do that quite a lot. Everyone dressed? Quick march."

"What do we do, Scarlet?" Lila asked as they followed Gilbert Gauntlet through the palm trees. The pirate henchmen followed close behind.

"Escape," Scarlet said, filled with determination.

"How?" said Melvin.

"Don't worry, crew," Scarlet said, lifting her chin. "I'll think of something."

"This is where you'll be today," Gilbert Gauntlet said.

They had stopped beside a long shack in the middle of the jungle. Inside the shack was a long conveyor belt. And standing behind the conveyor belt were thirty gloomy pirate trainees in purple T-shirts and caps. They all had brushes and paint pots. Small red squares of material were passing along the conveyor belt in front of them.

"What are they doing?" Lila asked.

"Painting spots on pirate bandanas, dear lady," said Gilbert Gauntlet.

"This isn't a pirate school," Scarlet said. "It's a pirate factory!"

"Nonsense," said Gilbert Gauntlet. "You're learning useful skills. That's what school's all about, girlie. In a couple of days you'll be on pirate hooks. Then parrot-catching at the weekend."

"Don't tell me," Scarlet said. "You sell everything and we don't see a penny?"

"Naturally," Gilbert Gauntlet said. "Now, take your places. Captain Curl will answer any questions."

"You're a foul-breathed fart-filled fruitcake, Gauntlet," One-Eyed Scott said.

"Farewell, my hearties," Gilbert Gauntlet said. "I'm off to my luxury yacht."

Scarlet didn't remember a luxury yacht in the harbour of Swashbuckle Island. Gilbert Gauntlet must have moored it somewhere else.

"And remember …" Gilbert Gauntlet struck a pose. "Ahoy, you scum and scurvy knaves – Gilbert Gauntlet rules the waves!"

"Toasted toenails!" Scarlet gasped, as Gilbert Gauntlet disappeared through the palm trees. "I know why I've heard of Gilbert Gauntlet. He did that advert on telly for a new marina he was building, about a year ago. He dressed up as a pirate for the advert, and that scurvy knave thing – it was his catchphrase!"

"Didn't that marina fall into the sea?" Lila asked.

"Two weeks after it opened," Scarlet said. "It made a very loud splash, sank fourteen boats and nearly drowned the poor mayor."

"I remember," Cedric gasped.

"And then the fellow disappeared," Melvin said, nodding. "It was in all the papers, wasn't it?"

"And now we're in his clutches,"

Grandpa Jack said sadly.

"Blithering bunions," said One-Eyed Scott.

On their first day at Swashbuckle School, the Silvers and One-Eyed Scott painted so many bandanas that Scarlet saw spots in her sleep. The next day, they dried, ironed and packed the bandanas in purple boxes. The day after that, they turned hundreds of old metal coat-hangers into pirate hooks. Now they were packing those into more purple boxes. Captain Curl and the rest of the henchmen patrolled the edges of the island, making sure that no one escaped. And Scarlet still didn't have a plan. Things were getting desperate.

Scarlet wondered what Long Joan Silver

would do in this situation. Then she
sighed. Long Joan Silver would never
have handed over the keys to *55 Ocean
Drive* in the first place.

"Uh oh," Cedric said.

Gilbert Gauntlet was strolling across
the sand towards them. Today he was
wearing a pinstriped hat with a large
purple feather stuck in the brim. One-
Eyed Scott muttered something so rude
that a lizard blushed and ran up a
nearby tree.

Gilbert Gauntlet stopped beside a towering pile of purple boxes.

Scarlet wondered if she could kick the

boxes and bring them down on Gilbert Gauntlet's head. But her foot was too far away from the bottom box.

"For the rest of the day, you will be catching parrots," Gilbert Gauntlet said. "Now, how will you do this?"

"Shoot them," suggested a goofy-toothed pirate trainee.

"What a stupid pupil you are," said Gilbert Gauntlet. "I want live parrots, not dead ones."

Scarlet remembered how Long Joan's parrot Lipstick had loved it when the family had played music and everyone had danced. Her mum and dad were nifty musicians. She stared at the sand. She wished her granny was here.

"Work it out amongst yourselves, you useless lot," Gilbert Gauntlet said. "I simply want them alive. I'm off to my luxury yacht for cocktails now. I will return in the morning."

The pirate trainees muttered to each other as Gilbert Gauntlet walked away.

Thinking about Lipstick had given Scarlet a plan. She put up her hand and smiled sweetly at Captain Curl.

"We want to use music to catch our parrots, Captain Curl, sir," she said. "But our instruments are on board our ship. We also need some banana-flavoured chewing gum from our kitchen cupboards. Can I fetch them please?"

"*I'll* fetch 'em," growled Captain Curl.

"Boiled bananas," said Scarlet as the henchman walked off. "He was supposed to let *me* go. Then I would have got our ship back."

She made another note in her head. *Never underestimate a pirate henchman.* Really, she would have to write down her

65

pirate notes soon or she'd forget them all.

Captain Curl returned with the Silvers' instruments and the chewing gum. There was Lila's accordion, and Melvin's mouth organ, and Grandpa Jack's tambourine.

"At least we can have a sing-song," said Cedric. "It might cheer us up."

"Chew this," Scarlet said, handing out the chewing gum. "We'll smear the gum on the branches of the trees. When the parrots land on the branches to listen to our music, they'll get stuck."

"Brilliant," Grandpa Jack said.

"It was Long Joan's idea," Scarlet said. "She used it to catch Lipstick."

The Silvers and One-Eyed Scott walked up the beach with their musical instruments and found a nice jungle clearing. Parrots flew overhead in a whirl of bright feathers as they smeared a few branches with the gum.

Lila put on her accordion. Melvin put his mouth organ to his lips.

"Play it, pirates," said Grandpa Jack as he lifted his tambourine.

They burst into their favourite song, *The Funky Eyepatch*. Soon, the whole family was dancing beneath the trees.

Suddenly there was a fluttering overhead. Scarlet saw a red parrot twirling in the air. The parrot was a fiery shade of red – the exact shade of Long Joan Silver's favourite lipstick.

The parrot landed on one of the sticky branches. Then it looked at the Silvers and One-Eyed Scott.

"Hello treasures," squawked Lipstick.

The Riddle

Lila screamed. Melvin gasped. Grandpa Jack and One-Eyed Scott goggled and Cedric sat down with a thud.

Scarlet stared at the parrot with wide eyes.

"Is it?" Lila whispered.

"It can't be," Melvin said.

"Long Joan always said 'hello treasures' when she saw us," said Cedric.

"It's the right shade of red for Lipstick,"

Scarlet said in excitement. "There's a feather missing from its tail, look. The feather in our keyring!"

"But Lipstick was eaten by the shrimp!" Grandpa Jack squeaked. "Same as Long Joan!"

The parrot that looked like Lipstick tried to fly off the branch, but his feet were well and truly stuck.

"Farting fruitbats," said Lipstick, looking at his feet in disgust.

"I taught him that!" One-Eyed Scott shouted, hopping up and down. "It's Lipstick! It really is!"

"Farting fruitbats," Lipstick said again, and cracked his beak.

Lila unstuck Lipstick's feet from the branch. The red parrot flapped and fluttered on Lila's arm, and nipped her

gently on the ear.

"Well," said Melvin, twisting his
moustache. "Well, well, well."

Scarlet picked a banana from a nearby
banana tree and peeled it. Bananas had

always been Lipstick's favourite food.

Lipstick nipped the end off the banana. He burped loudly

"Bit rude sorry," said Lipstick, sounding contented. "Farting fruitbats, rar!"

"How did you escape from the shrimp?" Lila asked, stroking Lipstick's feathers.

"I seed you get swallowed with my own eye," One-Eyed Scott said.

"I guess the shrimp spat you out," Scarlet said.

Everyone was silent. Scarlet knew they were all thinking the same thing.

It was a shame the shrimp hadn't spat out Long Joan as well.

Lipstick ate the rest of the banana. He closed his eyes.

Then he said something very strange.

"Underwater, overboard,
Up on high and wave the sword,
Solve the riddle at your leisure,
Come and find tremendous treasure."

Scarlet's heart beat very quickly. Had
Lipstick said *treasure*?

"Rollicking rhubarb," One-Eyed Scott
said. "'Tis a riddle."

"Long Joan must have taught Lipstick the riddle before the shrimp got her!" said Lila with a gasp.

"A treasure hunt!" shouted Cedric. "A real live treasure hunt!"

Dizzy with excitement, the Silvers and One-Eyed Scott hugged each other and danced on the spot. They twirled and whirled until they fell on to the sand, out of breath and laughing.

"Now all we have to do," Scarlet said, "is get off this island!"

Everyone agreed that they couldn't give Lipstick to Gilbert Gauntlet. So they concentrated on catching more parrots. The songs that Lila and Melvin played were livelier than they had been for a long time. Soon they had caught four parrots on the sticky branches. After giving the parrots some bananas, the Silvers and One-Eyed Scott sat down underneath a tree. Lipstick perched on Lila's shoulder.

"Here's the plan," Scarlet said. "We have to break into Gilbert Gauntlet's office tonight."

"What if Gauntlet sees us?" asked One-Eyed Scott.

"His luxury yacht is moored on the other side of the island," Scarlet said. "You can see it from our hut. The office is down by the harbour. We get the keys to *55 Ocean Drive*. Then we shake the sand of this island from our pirate boots and sail after the tremendous treasure!"

"We haven't worked out the riddle yet," Lila said.

"Underwater," said Lipstick brightly.

"Overboard. Up on high and wave the sword. Rar."

Was the treasure underwater *and* overboard, Scarlet wondered. Up on high could be anything, and sword-waving sounded dangerous. She had no idea what the riddle meant. But her crew was counting on her. She wouldn't let them down.

"We'll work on the riddle when we get back on board *55 Ocean Drive*," Scarlet said. "But we *have* to leave this place tonight, crew."

"It'll be dark tonight," Melvin said. "How will we see where we're going?"

"We'll follow the stars," said Grandpa Jack in a wise voice.

"I know all about the stars," Cedric said happily. He struck a Space Beard pose and starting doing his special moon walk across the sand.

One-Eyed Scott peered up at the sky. "We won't see no stars tonight," he said.

Dark clouds were rolling across the sun. A storm was coming.

That night, Scarlet and her family returned to their dingy hut, changed out of their horrible uniforms and tried to get some sleep. But the storm made sleep impossible. It screeched. It howled. It roared and shook and shivered. Ralph the cat hid at the bottom of Melvin's hammock. Bluebeard tucked his little head deep underneath his wing. Lipstick rocked on the edge of Lila's hammock and muttered "Farting fruitbats" a lot.

Suddenly there was a huge gust of wind. The hut's roof peeled away like the lid of a tin can and the rain lashed in. Soon, everyone was soaked.

"Really," said Lila as rain dripped off her nose. "That Gilbert Gauntlet can't even build a hut to withstand a measly little hurricane. And he calls himself a pirate!"

"I hope he and his luxury yacht get blown out to sea," Melvin said.

"Luxury yuck," said One-Eyed Scott.

Scarlet turned over in her hammock and tried to ignore the rain. She was still wondering about Lipstick's riddle. *Underwater, overboard …* Was it sunken treasure? Who was overboard? Her head hurt just thinking about it.

There was a crash of thunder. Ralph tried to climb inside Melvin's shirt.

Scarlet sighed. They couldn't attack Gilbert Gauntlet's office in this weather,

or sail away in *55 Ocean Drive*. Her plan
had failed once again.

Sadly, Scarlet decided she was a

rubbish pirate captain. She would ask
her crew to vote for someone else in the
morning.

6

Constipated Catfish

Everyone was very glad to see
the sun rise after the storm. Forgetting
about their uniforms, they rushed outside
to see the damage for themselves. The
sky looked like someone had scrubbed it
clean. There were no clouds, and the
breeze was warm and gentle. But
Swashbuckle Island was a different
matter. Palm trees lay across the beach.

Broken boxes scattered wet

pirate bandanas and pirate hooks across the sand. The parrot cages were smashed and the parrots had escaped.

"And I thought my *bedroom* was messy," said Cedric.

Scarlet took a deep breath.

"I need to tell you all something," she said.

"Where's Gilbert Gauntlet's luxury yacht?" Lila asked suddenly.

There was no sign of the yacht, which was usually moored a hundred metres from the beach.

"It *has* been blown out to sea!" said Melvin in delight.

Captain Curl and the other henchmen had noticed that the yacht was missing as well. They stood in a huddle and whispered in anxious voices.

Scarlet forgot all about resigning as captain. She had a plan.

She had seen that all the henchmen had their backs to the pirate trainees.

"Let's get out of here!" she said. The Silvers and One-Eyed Scott

began sneaking towards the trees. Some other pirate trainees started doing the same thing. Soon, everyone was running.

Ralph raced beside Scarlet. Bluebeard clung on to Scarlet's hat and Lipstick swooped overhead. Melvin carried Cedric, and Lila held hands with

Grandpa Jack and One-Eyed Scott. They
ran to their hut and collected their
instruments. Then they fled through
broken branches and tattered leaves.
They jumped over swampy puddles and
snoozing snakes. They ran and ran until
they reached the harbour on the other
side of the island.

Wonderfully, *55 Ocean Drive* was still afloat. So were all the other ships.

"Head for the office," said Scarlet. "Get the keys!"

"Wasn't the office over there?" Melvin asked, panting.

A broken pile of purple-painted planks lay in a heap on the beach. The swizzly chair had broken in half. The desk was upside down. The computer was smashed. The filing cabinet had spilled paper all over the beach. The quill was floating out to sea. And there was no sign of any keys at all.

Captain Curl and the other four henchman appeared on the beach. Scarlet seized a plank. "Don't come near us, Curlylocks!" she shouted, waving the plank. "Or I'll knock that stupid hat off

your bald head! As for the rest of you –
you'll be picking splinters out of your
bottoms for weeks!"

The others picked up planks and
started waving them as well.

The henchmen turned around and ran
back into the trees.

"They're scared of us!" Cedric said. "I'm
Space Beard the Scary!"

Scarlet tucked her purple plank into
her belt. "We have to find those keys,"
she said. "Get looking!"

Everyone hunted for the keys. Every now and then, Captain Curl and the henchmen tried to attack. Whenever this happened, the Silvers and One-Eyed Scott waved their purple planks and shouted "Garr!" in their fiercest pirate voices. Then Captain Curl and the henchmen squealed and disappeared into the trees again.

Slowly, keys began to appear.

There was a small one on a shark's tooth keyring hanging halfway up a palm tree, which fitted the fishing boat. Then they found a huge iron key on a gold doubloon, half-buried in the sand. This one fitted the galleon. There was a bunch of jingly silver ones on a whizzy silver plipper for the sporty speedboat, and a long golden key on a fish-shaped keyring for the tug. But the plastic-coated red-parrot-feather keyring was nowhere to be seen.

With lots of thanks and waving, the other pirate trainees began leaving the island. Soon Scarlet and her crew were the only pirate trainees left.

"Look!" Lila gasped, pointing out to sea.

Gilbert Gauntlet's luxury yacht was limping over the horizon. It didn't look very luxurious any more. Its gleaming white sides were bashed and battered. Its sails hung like rags on the masts. Gilbert Gauntlet was coming back to Swashbuckle Island.

"What are we going to do, Scarlet?" Cedric asked.

"I don't know," Scarlet said. She looked at Grandpa Jack. "What would Long Joan do, Grandpa Jack?"

"She'd tell you to keep your spirits up,

young Scarlet," said Grandpa Jack. "The Silvers never give up. Then she'd probably tell me to go fishing."

Grandpa Jack and One-Eyed Scott set up a fishing line on the edge of the harbour. Melvin and Lila got out their instruments and sang a sad song called *The Last of the Maltesers*. Cedric stroked Ralph, and Bluebeard and Lipstick swayed in time to the music.

Scarlet stared at *55 Ocean Drive*. They were so near to escaping, and yet still so far away. Her first pirate voyage had been a disaster. She *would* resign as soon as they had eaten their dinner.

Grandpa Jack soon caught a whiskery catfish. They made a fire on the beach and One-Eyed Scott prepared the dinner.

Gilbert Gauntlet's yacht was getting closer and closer. Scarlet could just make out the yacht's name now, *The Glove*, written in curly purple letters on the prow.

"Galloping gudgeons," said One-Eyed Scott suddenly.

"What?" Scarlet said in a grumpy voice.

"Christmas kippers and cheesy dippers!" said One-Eyed Scott.

"WHAT?" demanded the Silvers.

"Look what was inside our dinner!" said One-Eyed Scott.

The family gasped.

Lying in One-Eyed Scott's hand was a plastic-coated red-parrot-feather keyring.

"It's a plastic-coated red-parrot-feather keyring," said Scarlet stupidly.

Cedric's mouth fell open. "Are you saying that ... that catfish *ate* our keyring?" he said.

"Yup," said One-Eyed Scott.

"Wow!" Melvin shouted, dropping his mouth organ.

"Whee!" Lila yelled as her accordion went *squoing*.

One-Eyed Scott tossed Scarlet the keys to *55 Ocean Drive*.

"CONSTIPATED CATFISH!" Scarlet cried as she caught them. "Grandpa Jack caught the most important constipated catfish in the world! Quick! *Head for the ship!*"

The Silvers raced for the harbour.

Gilbert Gauntlet appeared on the deck of his yacht. His hat had lost its purple feather, and he looked ragged and furious. "You scum!" he shouted. "You scurvy knaves! No one leaves Swashbuckle Island without my permission!"

Scarlet leaped aboard *55 Ocean Drive*. She wanted to kiss the deck, but there wasn't time.

"Too late, Gauntlet, you corrugated cowpat!" shouted One-Eyed Scott, shinning up the ropes of *55 Ocean Drive* with Ralph the cat clinging around his shoulders.

"Yahoo!" Grandpa Jack yelled.

Melvin cartwheeled up the gangplank. Cedric flipped on his jumping springs and bounded aboard like a kangaroo. Lipstick and Bluebeard screeched in the blue sky as Scarlet heaved up the anchor. Grandpa Jack unfurled the sails. One-Eyed Scott tied his chicken bones back into his hair. Scarlet unlocked the ship's wheel with her keys and threw her pirate hat in the air with delight.

"We'll meet again!" Gilbert Gauntlet roared in rage.

"We can't wait!" Scarlet yelled, grinning as wide as the horizon. "But right now, we've got a riddle to solve and some treasure to find!"

And with a burst of *The Funky Eyepatch*, *55 Ocean Drive* sailed out to sea.

Mum and Dad

Cedric

One-Ey